For Gavin and Robbie, who collect with me,
and to all past and future collectors too.

www.mascotbooks.com

My Shoebox

For more information, please contact:
Mascot Books
620 Herndon Parkway, Suite 320
Herndon, VA 20170
info@mascotbooks.com

Library of Congress Control Number: 2021923303

CPSIA Code: PRT0222A

ISBN-13: 978-1-63755-224-7

Printed in the United States

My Shoebox

Laura Fleming
Illustrated by David Gnass

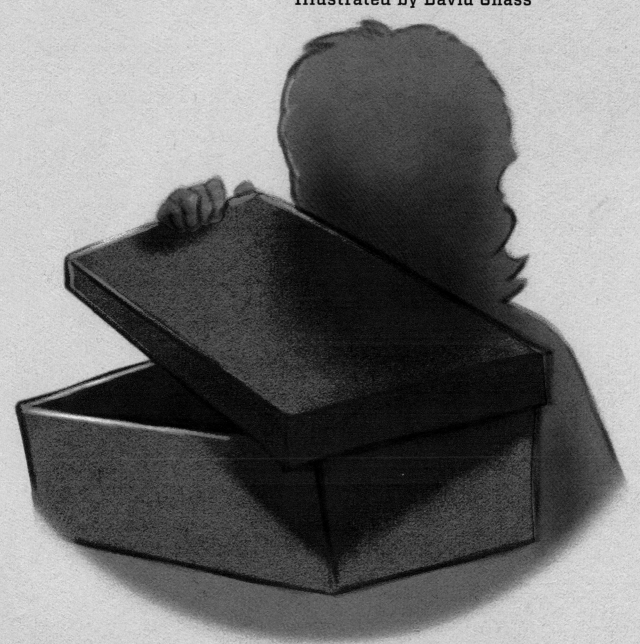

When I was young, I was given an empty shoebox. On every birthday or holiday, my parents would add something special to the shoebox, and it would get more and more full. I didn't really understand what the box was for, but everyone seemed happy and excited about it, so I was too.

Even though everyone was excited about my shoebox, it was kept on a shelf way up high in my closet. Every night as I laid in bed and drifted off to sleep, I would look up at the shelf and think, *wouldn't it be nice to see what was inside?*

One day, when I finally grew tall enough to reach the shelf, I stood on my tiptoes and carefully took my shoebox down.

I slowly opened the lid, peeked inside, and gasped at what I saw . . .

Inside the box were small pieces of cardboard, each with the familiar face of a professional sports player I loved!

One by one, I carefully took all of the cards out of my box. To my surprise, I saw Shohei Ohtani, Patrick Mahomes, Stephen Curry, and Sabrina Ionescu!

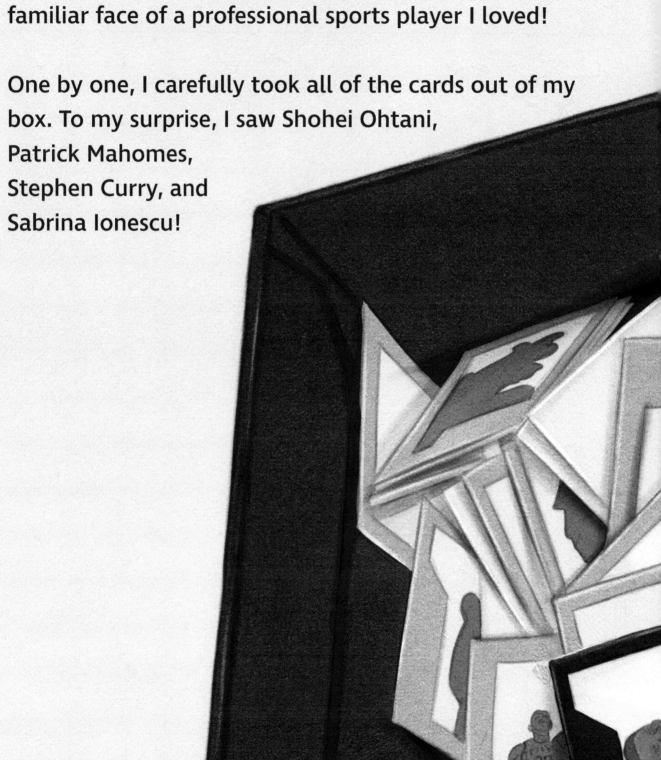

Sometimes, when I look at my sports cards, I dream of what it would be like to be a famous athlete. I could be a baseball player with a crisp, clean uniform and a flat-billed cap carrying a big wooden bat on my shoulder.

I could play basketball and swish the ball from the three-point line with one second left to win the game!

Or, hut . . . hut . . . hike! I could experience
the thrill of throwing the game-winning
touchdown pass to win the Super Bowl!

I'd have sports cards made of me that other kids would collect in their own shoeboxes.

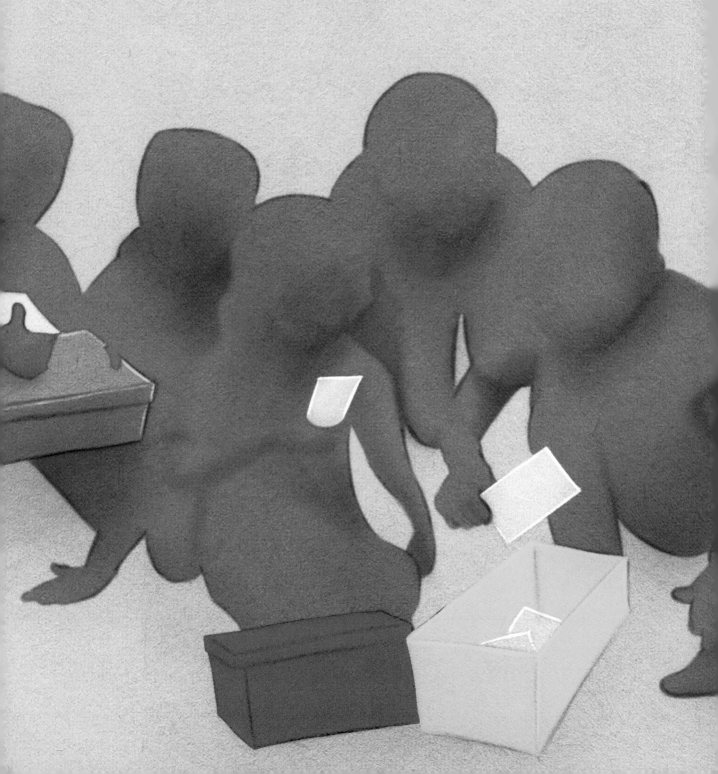

Now that I am older,

I understand what makes
my shoebox so special,

and I get just as excited about it as the rest of my family.

Sometimes, I get cards of my favorite players, and sometimes I don't, but I still add each and every one of them to my shoebox. I love them all.

Every child in my family has been given their own shoebox. Someday, when my child is old enough, I will give them their own shoebox to keep on a tall shelf and fill with special cards.

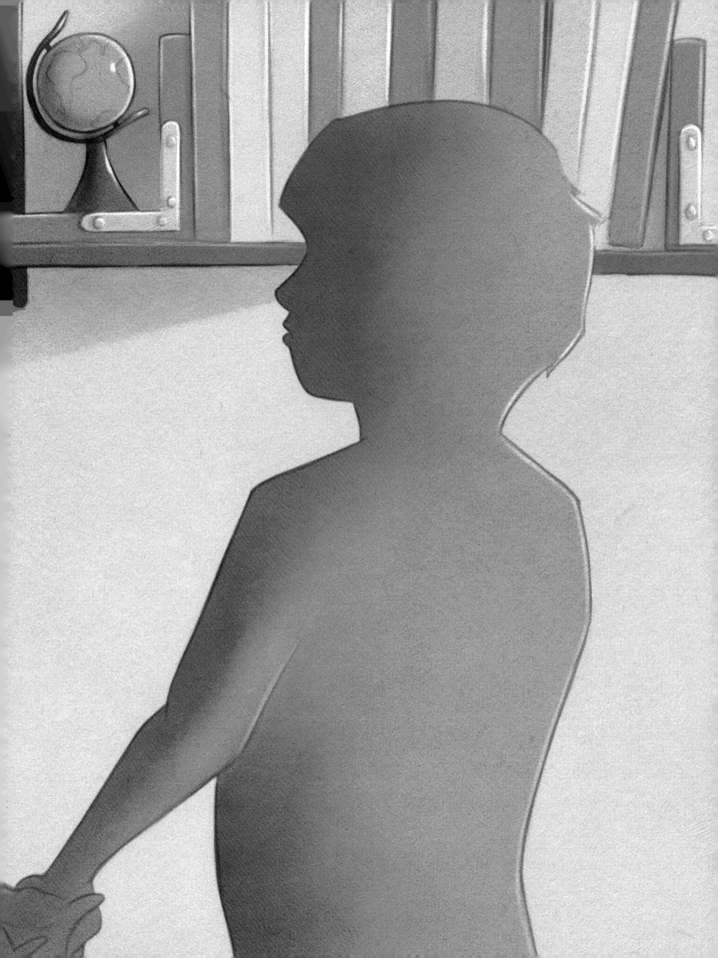

About the Author

Laura Fleming is an educator of twenty-five years and is the bestselling author of two education books for teachers. She is a mom to the most wonderful boy on the planet and has been an avid sports card collector her whole life.